The Pony That Nobody Wanted

by Lurlene McDaniel

illustrated by Dennis E. Miller
cover illustration by Bill Robison

Published by Willowisp Press, Inc.
401 E. Wilson Bridge Road, Worthington, Ohio 43085

Printed in the United States of America

10 9 8 7 6 5 4

ISBN 0-87406-074-5

One

Holly Hunter knew it was going to be a bad day from the minute she got out of bed. First, she stubbed her toe on her skate board. She could have sworn she had put it away in her closet the night before. Next, she remembered Miss Tucker was giving a spelling test. And finally, when she went down to breakfast, Holly discovered her mother had fixed oatmeal.

Ugh! Holly hated oatmeal. It looked so ugly—all lumpy and thick. "Now, eat fast," Mrs. Hunter had urged. "You're late and the school bus will be here in fifteen minutes."

Holly stirred the stuff in her bowl. She watched her mom fixing her lunch for school. The big, old farm kitchen was warm and sunny. It smelled like fresh cinnamon.

"Hi, honey." Holly's dad appeared in the room. He kissed his wife and patted Holly on her head.

3

"How's my favorite girl?" Tim Hunter asked. He sat down next to Holly and drank his orange juice.

Holly smiled at her father. He was the most handsome man in the world to her. "Fine," Holly sighed. She took a bite of toast.

"You look like you've lost your best friend," he teased.

Holly thought of Patsy. At least she would be riding to school with her best friend. Then she remembered that Patsy was sick with a cold. That meant Holly would have to face a whole day of school with Butch Moffat—alone. Her appetite totally disappeared.

"I've got a spelling test today," she told her dad.

"Did you study?"

"A little." Holly squirmed in her chair. She should have said, "Not much."

"What did you do last night before bed?" he asked.

"Read a horse story," her mother said, setting scrambled eggs down in front of him.

"Oh, Holly . . ." he began.

"But I *like* horse stories!" Holly cried. "Oh, Dad, I want a horse of my own more than anything!"

Her dad sighed. "Now, Holly, we've been over

and over it. Horses cost a lot of money. And besides you're only ten."

"But we have lots of room for a horse," Holly said. It was true. Her father was the minister for the whole area. And their home, the parsonage, was right next to the old wooden church building where everyone came for Sunday services.

The old farm house they lived in had five acres of land around it—plenty of beautiful, rich pasture land—a small stable and corral, a hen house, and in the summer, a big vegetable garden.

"And I'll work hard at my chores to earn money," Holly said excitedly. "Why, I could help you harvest the honey hives, and clean the church every week and . . ."

"Hold on, young lady," her dad laughed. "Yes, we have plenty of room for a horse. But a horse costs too much to buy. And you have to take care of it. Maybe when you're older . . ."

It always ended the same way. ". . . maybe when you're older . . . too much money . . ."

Suddenly, she heard the school bus blowing its horn at the front of the yard.

"You're late!" her mother cried. Holly jumped up, grabbed her books and lunch box and kissed her parents good-bye. She ran down the front porch steps. Holly struggled with her jacket in the cool spring air. She was out of breath when she got on the bus. She took her seat and opened her notebook. Inside was a horse magazine. Holly thumbed through it. She loved all the pictures of the beautiful horses. Well, someday she'd have her very own horse—just like Butch Moffat.

It wasn't fair that Butch should have a horse and not her. He was ten also. But his father let Butch have a horse. Holly thought about Butch's pinto horse. His name was Tonto. And Holly thought he was the most wonderful horse. Of course, she'd never let Butch know it. He was so stuck-up about it. But Tonto had won lots of ribbons and trophies in rodeos. Butch rode Tonto in barrel races and won all the time.

Holly watched the farm countryside go by from her seat by the window. The signs of spring were everywhere. Bright green grass pushed through the ground. New leaves were on the trees. Mrs. Smith's tulip patch was full of blooming flowers. Yes, Holly's life would be perfect . . . if only she had a horse.

* * * * * *

"Hey! What's the matter, Holly? You got the measles?" Holly chewed hard on her sandwich and tried to ignore Butch's words. "Oh, I see now," Butch said in a loud voice. "It's not really measles ... just lots of freckles." Butch and his friend Todd Farner laughed. Dumb boys! Holly thought.

Sally Cutler slid over next to Holly. "That mean old Butch," she said to Holly. "Don't pay any attention to him."

Holly smiled at Sally. Holly was glad she'd sat with Sally. Why did Patsy have to be sick anyway? "It's OK," she told Sally. "I'm used to Butch."

Holly watched as Butch and Todd left the schoolroom. The school was too small for a cafeteria, so everybody ate lunch at their desks. Then they went outside and played.

"I'll be glad when school's out for the summer," Sally said.

"Yeah, just a few more months," Holly agreed. Then she'd have a whole summer to think about having her own horse. She and Patsy could run around the corral and pretend they were riding fast

7

race horses.

Later, Holly waited for her school bus home. She was still daydreaming when the bus pulled up. Holly stepped up for the step, when she felt an awful tug on the back of her dress. "Oh!" she cried. Her books fell all over the ground. The sash on her dress dangled behind her. And all she could hear was the loud laughter of Butch.

"Have a nice trip?" he howled.

"You leave me alone!" Holly shouted at him. She was so angry. "I almost fell!" Angrily, she picked up her books. She got on the bus. But she could still hear him laughing. "Darn him anyway!" Holly thought. Someday she was going to punch him out.

Holly felt ashamed of herself. She knew she wasn't supposed to think thoughts like that. But Butch was so mean to her.

"What a day," Holly thought. "A stubbed toe, oatmeal, a spelling test and Butch Moffat. What other bad things could happen?"

As the bus bounced along the road home, Holly thought things couldn't get worse.

Two

After Holly changed into her jeans and put away her school clothes, she went to the kitchen for some cookies and milk.

"Did you have a good day at school?" her mother asked. She was peeling vegetables at the sink.

"Fine," Holly sighed. "I wish Patsy was well," Holly added.

"I talked to her mother today. She said she'd be back in school by tomorrow," Mrs. Hunter said.

"Good!" Holly said. That made her feel better. "Where's Dad?" Holly asked.

"In his study. He's working on Sunday's sermon," her mother said.

Just then they heard a car honk its horn. "Who's that?" Holly asked. She jumped up and ran to the kitchen window.

Outside, she could see the big brown station wagon of Mrs. Moffat stopping in front of the church. "I'm sure it's Mrs. Moffat," Holly's mother

10

said. "She called earlier and asked if she could come over and practice some new music on the church organ."

Holly groaned. Mrs. Moffat was the church organist. And if she'd come over to practice, it meant Butch was with her. Sure enough, Holly saw them both get out of the car. Oh, no! Holly thought. Won't I ever get rid of him?

"Hello!" Holly's mother called through the window.

"Hi, Sara!" Mrs. Moffat called back.

Butch kicked up a wad of dirt. It flew into the air and scattered into a million bits of dust. "Stop that this instant!" his mother said. Then she turned to Mrs. Hunter and said, "I'm going on inside the church and get started!"

"Fine!" Sara Hunter called back. "When you're finished, come over and have some tea."

"Thanks!" she said. Then she went into the old church building.

Butch stood around outside the church kicking up dust. I've got to go hide, Holly thought.

"Why don't you go play with Butch for a while?" her mother asked.

"I-I-I've got homework," Holly said.

"There's plenty of time for that," her mother smiled. "I mean, as crazy as you are about horses ... and Butch with his very own horse ... well, I would think you two would have lots to talk about."

Holly rolled her eyes. How could she ever tell her mother how she really felt about Butch?

"I'm going upstairs for a minute," said Mrs. Hunter. "Now you go on outside and play with Butch. He looks lonely."

He looked lonely, all right. But who'd want to hang out with a skunk? Holly thought as she turned away from the window. Now what was she going to do?

Suddenly her eyes fell on the peeled vegetables. She got an idea. She picked up one of the vegetables and turned it over carefully. Yes. It almost looked like a peeled apple. Holly rinsed it off real good. Then she went out onto the porch.

Butch came walking over. "Hi, freckles!" he grinned.

"That was a mean thing you did to me today," Holly said. "I could have been hurt when you pulled my sash. Besides, you almost tore my new dress."

"Aw, who cares?" Butch said. Then he noticed the food in her hand. "What's that?" he asked.

"An apple," Holly said. "My mom peeled it for me." She stepped past him and headed toward the old corral.

"Let me have a bite," Butch demanded.

"Fat chance," Holly said. She stood up on the wooden rail of the corral fence. Holly tossed the "fruit" into the air and caught it again.

"Just one bite," Butch said. "Mom hurried me over here. I didn't have time to eat anything."

Holly could hear the rich sounds of the organ playing. They were far from the kitchen window. "Tough," she said. Then she tossed the "apple" into the air again.

With one quick motion, Butch grabbed at it. He caught it and jumped down off the fence. "I got it now!" he yelled.

"You give that back to me right now!" Holly cried.

But he ignored her and ran off. He never saw the smile cross her face. Holly hurried back to her house. She darted inside and bounded up the stairs to her room. Even though she closed the bedroom door, she still heard Butch yell.

Must have bitten into the "apple," Holly thought. Serves him right, for the way he treated me today.

13

She bet he'd be more careful next time he took food from her. Since the "apple" was really a big fat potato! Holly could hear him wailing away below her bedroom window.

"Holly!" she heard her mother yell. "Holly Hunter! You come down here this minute!"

Holly took a deep breath. She could hear Butch carrying on in her hallway. "Coming, Mom!" Holly yelled back. Then she squared her shoulders and went to the door. She knew she was going to get into trouble. That was for sure. But it had been worth it.

* * * * * *

After supper, Holly helped her mother clear the table. She helped dry the dishes and put them away. Her dad sat reading while they worked. He had been angry with her. But he had been mad at Butch, too, for taking the potato from her in the first place.

Anyway, Mrs. Moffat had made Butch sit in the church while she practiced, and Holly had been sent to her room.

Once the dishes were finished, Holly went back upstairs to her room. She stared at her math

15

homework for a few minutes. Then she picked up one of her horse magazines and started looking through it.

It was filled with picture pages of beautiful horses. Palaminos, pintos, quarter horses . . . each was more beautiful than the last. Why did Butch have to have a horse and not her?

Suddenly, Holly stopped turning pages. She saw a full page advertisement. It said: "Adopt a Wild Horse or Burro."

Funny, she'd looked through that magazine before. Yet she'd never seen that ad. Eagerly, Holly read more.

> You can become a foster parent in a special government adoption program. Right now, the Bureau of Land Management is rounding up 250 wild horses—mustangs and burros—from the western plains and trucking them to Tennessee to be adopted by horse lovers on its Adopt-a-Horse program. Yes, the law requires that the number of these wild animals be reduced each year on the open range. That means that unless they are adopted, they must be killed.

Holly stopped reading. Her eyes filled with tears. How awful! All those wonderful horses. And nobody wanted them! She quickly read on.

Now, you can own one of these spirited horses
yourself. If you're approved by the government
and if you're willing to pay just $350, one of these
wild ponies or burros can be yours. Just fill out the
coupon below and mail it today.

Holly stopped reading again. Her heart was
pounding. Only $350! Why, most horses cost so
much more! Maybe . . . just maybe . . .

Holly jumped off her bed. She ran from her
bedroom and down the stairs two at a time. "Dad,
Mom!" she cried. "I can get my own horse! Look!
Look at this! My own horse! My very own horse!"

Three

"Well, this does look very interesting, Holly," Pastor Hunter said.

Holly stood next to her father's chair in his study. She was very excited. She watched as he read the advertisement. "Do you think we could do it?" Holly asked. She felt like she were going to pop from excitement.

"Honey," her dad began. "I just don't know. I mean, it's a good deal on a horse. But, Holly, they're wild horses. You can't just bring one home and hop on its back and ride it."

"I know that!" Holly said. "But we could train it together."

"I don't know anything about breaking and training a horse," her dad said.

"But Daddy! You know about everything!" Holly told him.

He laughed. "Not quite everything," he said. "I'd

18

have to talk to someone who owns horses. You know, find out how hard it's going to be."

Holly's heart pounded. He hadn't said no! "Oh, Daddy, there're lots of people in our church who know about horses."

"Yes . . ." he said slowly. "There's Mr. Moffat. Doesn't his boy, Butch, have some sort of rodeo horse?"

At the mention of Butch, Holly saw a dark cloud over her lovely plans. "Yes," she said.

"I suppose I could talk to him," her dad said.

"Sure!" Holly nodded. "Mr. Moffat knows a lot." Holly had always liked the Moffats. It was Butch she couldn't stand.

"OK, young lady," Pastor Hunter said as he hugged Holly. "I'll talk to Mr. Moffat and we'll write away for more information."

"Oh, Dad! Thank you! Thank you!" Holly clapped her hands and jumped happily.

"Now, don't get all excited," he warned her. "I didn't say 'yes.' I said I'd check into it more carefully."

But Holly was satisfied. In just a little time, she might have her very own horse.

* * * * * *

"Your own horse?" Patsy stared wide-eyed at Holly across the see-saw. "You're going to get your own horse?"

Holly had been saving up her big "news" all morning. The minute she saw Patsy at school the next day, she had wanted to tell her. But Holly kept her secret to herself. She kept her secret until after lunch. She waited until they were outside during lunch recess. Then she told her best friend her wonderful news.

"Can I ride it?" Patsy asked.

"Well, nobody can ride it at first," Holly said. "But after Dad and I tame it, of course, you can ride it."

Patsy shouted happily. "What will you name it?"

"Oh, I don't know," Holly said. "I think I'd have to see it first before I could think up a good name."

"When will you get it?" Patsy asked.

Holly looked down at the ground. "Oh, I'm not sure when the shipment arrives." She didn't want to say that her dad had only said maybe she could have a horse.

All at once, Holly felt a sting in the middle of her

back. "Ouch!" she cried.

"You stop that, Butch Moffat!" Patsy yelled.

Holly twisted around on the see-saw in time to see Butch and Todd take off running. He'd hit her in the back with a spitball.

"Are you all right?" Patsy asked.

"Fine," Holly said. Her back stung. But nothing was going to get her down today, not even Butch Moffat.

* * * * * *

When Holly got home from school, Mr. Moffat was talking to her father in his study. How she wished she could be in the room listening! Her mother made her sit in the kitchen and eat a snack. But Holly could hardly swallow. How she prayed that Mr. Moffat would say adopting a wild horse was a good idea.

Finally, he left. Pastor Hunter came into the kitchen. He sat across from her at the table. Holly stared at him. She felt very nervous.

"Mr. Moffat said that it takes a lot of work to train a horse. But he also said it was very rewarding."

Holly clapped her hands. "I knew we could do it!" she cried.

"Whoa! Slow down, young lady. We have to send off for all the forms first."

Holly could hardly wait. Her father also said, "What do you plan to do with your horse, Holly? Just ride it around here?"

"Oh, no," Holly said. "I want to ride it in rodeos. I want to take it to the Spring Festival next spring and ride in the barrel races. We can win lots of prizes and ribbons. I just know it."

Pastor Hunter threw back his head and laughed. "Holly Hunter! Why, you don't even have a horse yet and already you're counting the trophies you're bringing home!"

Holly blushed. "Well, it's fun to dream about," she said.

"I guess so," her dad said. "So, go ahead and dream."

* * * * * *

Every day, Holly rushed home from school and checked the mailbox. Every day, she called her friend Patsy and said, "Nothing new." But finally, nine days later, the special envelope came.

She watched eagerly as her parents read the letter from the Office of Land Management in Washington, D.C. Finally, her father explained everything to her.

"Holly, it says that our application must be back in one week. They're bringing the wild horses to a big ranch in Tennessee in just three weeks. We'd have to drive there to pick it up."

Holly listened very hard. "But we don't have a horse trailer," she said.

"Mr. Moffat said we could use his if we needed it," he said. "It also says that we have to prove that we have a good place to keep it."

That was easy, Holly thought. Their farm was perfect. The corral and small stable needed fixing up. But they could work on it together.

"It also says that you can't really own the horse for one year after you adopt it. At the end of a year's time, a veterinarian must come out and check the horse over. Then he must sign a form saying you've taken good care of the horse."

"Oh, I'll take real good care of it!" Holly cried.

"It's a big responsibility, Holly," Pastor Hunter warned.

"But I can do it, Daddy. If you're helping me, I know I can do it."

Mrs. Hunter nodded. "Then all we have to do is fill out the form. If we're approved, you'll have a horse."

Four

Holly couldn't sit still. The car seemed to be moving very slowly. But it wasn't. She wished she could go to sleep. It was dark outside. But she was too excited. She sat in the back seat of the family car and stared out the window. It was too dark to see. But the countryside was flying by.

She looked out the back window and could make out the huge shape of the horse trailer that bounced along behind them. It was empty now. But in just a few hours, it would hold her very own horse.

Holly remembered filling out the form. "It says we can ask for whatever horse we want," Pastor Hunter had said. "Mr. Moffat said we should ask for a filly about four years old. He thinks that would be the easiest to break and train for riding."

Sure, Holly had nodded. A filly. A girl just like me, Holly thought now as the car sped along. What would she name it? She and Patsy had written down lots of names. But Holly couldn't decide on one.

She knew she'd have to see the horse first. Then a name would pop into her mind.

Her mom and dad sat in the front seat. It was a ten-hour drive to the pick-up point in Tennessee from their farm. But Holly was so glad they were going that she never asked once, "How much longer?" or "Are we there yet?"

Finally, the sun came up. The green rolling hills of Tennessee were very pretty. The sun rose over the hills, and the road stretched ahead of them like a winding ribbon.

They arrived at the ranch at three o'clock in the afternoon. Holly was very tired. But she was so excited, she almost jumped from the car the minute it stopped.

"Hi, folks," a tall man said as he walked over to them. "I'm Bill Simpson," he said. "I'm with the Bureau of Land Management."

Pastor Hunter showed him their forms of approval to pick up their horse. The man nodded and led them to a big corral. Many horses shuffled around inside.

Holly stared wide-eyed at them. They looked hot and dusty—not all sleek and beautiful like the horses in her magazines.

"A fine, healthy bunch of mustangs," Mr. Simpson was saying. Holly felt a little disappointed. They all looked so . . . so . . . ordinary. And not very "wild" either, she thought.

"They've had a hard trip. They're tired," Mr. Simpson explained. "And some of them are pretty used to us humans already. Now, just wait here a minute, and let me get some of my men to cut your horse out of the herd."

Holly remembered that every horse was branded with a special government mark. And a special number that matched the one on their form would tell Mr. Simpson's men which horse was theirs.

Holly strained to see through the clouds of dust. Pretty soon, two men came through a gate into the corral. They were leading a small dusty, red-colored horse by two ropes around her neck.

"Here she is!" said Mr. Simpson.

A roan! Holly thought. She imagined all the dust and dirt washed off. She could see a gleaming red coat and flowing red mane and tail, too. "Flame!" Holly said aloud. Her eyes were shining with eagerness. "That will be your name. Flame!"

* * * * * *

Once they loaded the horse into the trailer and signed all the papers, it was late afternoon. But they headed back for home.

"So, what do you think of her?" Holly's mother asked her on the ride home.

"I think she's wonderful!" Holly sighed.

"You know, I've been doing a lot of reading about these mustangs since I said you could have one," Pastor Hunter told Holly. "Did you know that the word mustang means 'running free'?"

"No," Holly said. "What else did you read?"

"Well, they're descendants of horses that Cortez brought over when he discovered Mexico and the western United States."

Holly was very interested. She thought about history in school and remembered that Cortez was a Spanish explorer.

28

"The Indians had never seen a horse until Cortez brought them over from Spain," her dad said.

"Really?" Holly asked. "I thought horses always lived out West."

"Nope," he said. "America never had any horses until the explorers came. Then some got loose. Soon the Indians started riding them. Whole herds roamed on the plains. Some of the mustangs later became Pony Express runners."

Holly knew that in the Old West, the Pony Express carried the mail between cities and towns.

"Some became bucking broncos in Wild West Shows," Pastor Hunter continued. "And some just became cow ponies and saddle ponies. Now, the government is trying to re-locate them from all the grazing land out West. I think that this Adopt-a-Horse program is a pretty good one."

"So do I!" Holly said happily. "Now, I have my very own pony."

"Well, the wild mustangs eat a lot of grass that the ranchers need to feed to their cattle," her dad explained.

"So what?" Holly said. "I'm glad. Because now I have a pony that nobody wanted out West. A pony that nobody wanted . . . except me."

Five

"Isn't she beautiful?" Holly and Patsy stood on the bottom rail of the corral fence and watched Flame. The horse stood on the far side of the corral and ate some grass.

"She's kind of small," Patsy said. "And her hair is so long."

"Well, she's losing her winter coat," Holly said to her best friend.

"I wish we could pet her," Patsy said.

"I wish we could, too," Holly sighed. "But she doesn't trust us yet. Mr. Moffat said we have to win her confidence."

"How do we do that?" Patsy asked.

"Dad said by just hanging around. And always showing up at the same time to feed her. And bringing her sugar and pieces of apple. You know, stuff like that."

"How long before you can ride her?"

Holly hated all of Patsy's questions. She wished things could move along a little faster, too. It was hard to own a horse and not be able to ride it—or even pet it. But Flame would have nothing to do with Holly yet. Every time she moved near the horse, it turned and trotted to the other side of the corral.

"It takes time," Mr. Moffat told Holly and her dad. But Holly knew she didn't have TOO much time—not if she were going to ride Flame in the Spring Festival barrel race and beat Butch and Tonto.

Soon, Holly's life settled into a routine. She'd get up and get dressed for school. Then she would go down to the stable and corral and offer Flame her morning oats.

Flame liked to eat, but she wouldn't come over to the fence for Holly. So Holly would dump the oats into the feed box and go off to school.

After school, Holly would come home and try to offer Flame apples and goodies from her hand. But the horse wouldn't come near her.

Holly became discouraged. All anyone ever said to her was, "It takes time." Mr. Moffat came over and talked to her father about Flame. He said things were "progressing nicely." But to Holly's way of thinking, they weren't.

One day, Holly realized that there were only two weeks of school left. Oh, boy! she thought. Then she'd have all summer to work with Flame. The Spring Festival was always in the springtime. Maybe if she worked all summer and winter, Flame would be ready for the Festival by next spring. She hoped so, especially after the way Butch had made fun of Flame.

"You call that a horse?" he jeered one afternoon. His mother was practicing on the organ inside the church. Butch leaned over the fence. Holly stood next to him. She felt her cheeks grow red with anger.

"She's a great horse," Holly said. "Even your father thinks so!"

"I'll bet Tonto can run rings around her."

"I have to train her first," Holly said. "But she's a real mustang. And I'll bet she's fast as lightning."

"You mean slow as molasses!" Butch laughed.

Butch made Holly so mad. But there was nothing she could say—not yet, anyway. "Hey, look," Butch said, pointing at Flame. "She likes the music."

Sure enough. Flame had stopped grazing and

was staring off in the direction of the church. Her ears were pricked forward. She seemed to be listening. "You're right," Holly said softly. And suddenly she had a wonderful idea.

* * * * * *

The next morning was Saturday. Holly got dressed quickly and went down to the corral. She tucked her "special idea" inside her shirt pocket. Then Holly filled a bucket with oats and put the bucket inside the fence. Holly slipped through the bars of the fence and sat down next to the bucket.

Flame trotted to the other side of the corral. Holly ignored the horse. She reached inside her pocket and took out her portable pocket radio. Holly hunted around the dial until she heard a station playing soft music. Then she turned the volume up and sat very still.

Out of the corner of her eye, Holly could see Flame prick up her ears. She could see Flame staring over at her and the bucket of oats. Holly just sat very still.

It seemed like forever. But, finally, Flame came a few steps closer. Holly didn't move a muscle. The music played on and on. Flame came a little closer.

At last, Flame was only a few steps away. Holly could feel her heart pounding. She had never been so close to her horse!

Flame snorted and sniffed at the bucket of oats. But she kept coming closer. The music acted like a magnet. Finally, Flame was standing right next to Holly! Slowly, slowly, the horse bent down her nose and nibbled at the side of the bucket. Then she stuck her nose inside the bucket and ate some oats.

All the while, the music played. Holly could hardly breathe. Her muscles felt cramped, but she didn't move. She didn't want to scare Flame away with any sudden movement.

Then, very quietly, Holly began to talk. "Hi, Flame," she said. Flame jerked her head up. But she didn't run off. Holly tried to make her voice match the music. She spoke softly and soothingly. Flame continued to eat.

Holly told her horse everything she could think of. She told her about Patsy, about school, about Butch and Tonto—everything. And Flame seemed to listen. Even after she was finished eating, Flame just stood there and listened.

Slowly, Holly stretched out her hand. In it was a lump of sugar. Flame snorted and sniffed at it. She backed up. Then she reached over and licked the lump of sweetness out of Holly's hand. Then Flame trotted away.

Holly was so happy she felt like singing. Flame had actually come close to her! She'd eaten a lump of sugar from her hand. It was the first step in building up trust.

Holly remembered how warm and soft Flame's nose and breath had felt on her hand. "Oh, Flame," Holly sighed. "You're so wonderful!"

Six

"Good for you, Holly!" Pastor Hunter said. Holly had told him about the music and how Flame had stood next to her to eat her morning feed. "That's a very big step in breaking her. Keep up the good work."

Holly told Patsy that day at school, too. Patsy asked, "Can I come over this afternoon and watch?"

"Sure," Holly said. She couldn't wait to get home from school and try to get near Flame again.

That afternoon, while Patsy watched, Holly again filled the bucket with feed and sat next to it inside the corral. Holly turned up her pocket radio and waited for Flame. Sure enough, the horse came over and ate. Then Holly offered Flame another sugar cube. Flame ate it, too.

Every day after that, Holly did the same thing. In a week, Flame would trot over to the fence whenever she saw Holly. Soon, Holly didn't even have to bring the radio. Flame always came over looking for her food. Flame even let Holly pet her and scratch behind her ears.

One day Holly's father said, "I talked with Mr. Moffat. He said that since Flame trusts you now, it's time we put a halter on her."

School was over for the year, and it was a bright, sunny summer day. Holly knew that a halter was the first step in getting Flame to accept riding gear. A halter is a strap made of leather which fits over the horse's head. A halter would let Holly snap a rope to Flame to hold her in one place so she couldn't run off.

Mr. Moffat came over and gave Holly and Pastor Hunter instructions about putting a halter on Flame for the first time. Holly listened very carefully. She was going to have to slip it over Flame's head. She wanted to do it right.

Holly practiced on Tonto. Butch didn't like Holly messing with his horse one bit. But his father made him.

Tonto was much bigger than Flame. "A REAL horse," Butch said. Holly had to stand on her very tiptoes to reach his head. Secretly, Holly was glad Flame wasn't as big. It would be easier to put the halter on her.

Holly thought she was ready to try. She walked over to the corral fence. She had sugar in one hand and the halter in the other. Flame pricked up her ears when she saw Holly. Holly whistled for Flame. Flame trotted over.

Holly gave Flame a cube of sugar. Then she showed the halter to Flame. Flame sniffed at it. But she was more interested in the sugar. Then Holly rubbed the halter on Flame's neck. She didn't seem to mind.

Holly offered another lump of sugar to Flame. Then she quickly slipped the halter over Flame's ears and under her muzzle. Flame jerked back with a start. She shook her head. But the halter stayed on. Flame didn't like the halter, but she couldn't get it off. Holly held out another cube of sugar. Soon Flame forgot about the halter and trotted off.

"Very good!" her father and Mr. Moffat called. "That's the sign of a good horse," Mr. Moffat told Holly. "She's going to be very easy to break to saddle riding. And she'll be a fine and gentle animal, too."

Holly smiled broadly. Butch stuck out his tongue. "What's next?" her dad asked.

"Next we hook a rope to the halter and train her to walk and trot around in a big circle while Holly holds the rope. After that, we'll put a saddle blanket on her back. Then Holly can try sitting on her back on just the blanket. That's the biggest part— getting her to accept a rider."

Holly felt like singing. In just a little while, she'd be able to ride her horse. She could hardly wait.

* * * * * *

It was very early one morning. Holly was only half asleep. She heard a lot of noise. It was her father and mother talking. Then Holly heard them knocking on her bedroom door.

"Holly! Holly!" her mother shouted. "Come quick! Someone left the gate open. Flame's run away!"

Holly jumped out of bed in a flash. "What?" she cried. She ran to the door and flung it open.

Her mother looked very worried. "Flame's not in the corral. Dad's gone down to look around. But she's not in the stable either."

Holly didn't even bother to put on clothes over her nightgown. She just took off running. She got to

the corral and ran into her dad. "Holly!" he said
sternly. "Didn't you lock the gate last night?"

Holly felt like crying. "I thought I did," she said.

"Well, Flame's missing. Somehow she got out."

"Oh, Dad! We've got to find her! We just have
to!" Holly strained to see in the early morning haze.
Where was her beautiful Flame? What was going to
happen to her?

40

Seven

By nine o'clock in the morning, Holly had looked everywhere she could think of. Still, she had not found Flame. Her father called Mr. Moffat. He said he and Butch would come right over and help look.

"I just hope she hasn't taken off down the highway," Pastor Hunter said to Mr. Moffat. "I sure don't want her to get hit by a car."

Poor Flame. Holly was so worried about her. In her corral she had been safe. But wandering around she could get herself hurt. After all, she *was* a wild mustang. She didn't know anything about fast trucks and barbed wire fences.

Holly wanted to cry. But she didn't have time. She was too busy looking. She prayed while she looked for Flame. She prayed that God would keep Flame safe until they found her.

Butch rode off across the pasture land on Tonto. Holly wished she could go that far. Mr. Moffat and

41

Pastor Hunter rode all over to neighboring farms in a jeep. They asked friends and neighbors if they had seen Flame.

By lunch time they still had not found her. Mrs. Hunter made everybody come in for some sandwiches. Holly hated to stop looking. But she was hungry.

"Don't be too worried, Holly," Mr. Moffat said. "I think she'll wander back when she gets hungry enough."

"What if the Land Office finds out?" Holly asked suddenly.

"What do you mean?" her dad asked.

"You know," Holly continued. "The forms said they could take the horse back if we didn't take good care of her."

"Is that worrying you, too?" Pastor Hunter asked.

"It sure is," said Holly.

"Well, just as long as she doesn't get hurt, I think it will be all right."

"I thought Flame was your horse?" Butch asked between bites.

"She is!" Holly said hotly.

"Calm down," said Pastor Hunter. "Actually,

Butch, the Adopt-a-Horse program says that we can't really own Flame until we've kept her for one year. Then a vet must say that we've taken good care of the horse before the government will let us have full ownership."

"Look!" Holly's mother cried. She was pointing out her kitchen window. "It's Flame! And she's eating my garden!"

Everyone jumped up and ran outside. Sure enough. There was Flame. Right in the middle of the corn stalks.

"Flame! Flame!" Holly yelled.

"Careful!" Mr. Moffat warned. "Don't scare her."

Flame picked up her head and looked over at the cluster of people. But she kept right on chewing.

"She's ruining my garden!" Mrs. Hunter cried.

"But she's hungry," said Holly.

"Get out of my garden!" Sara Hunter cried.

"Don't scare her!" Pastor Hunter said again.

"Scare her!" said Mrs. Hunter. "I'm going to strangle her!"

"Mommy, please!" Holly pleaded.

Flame kept right on munching. The neat rows of corn lay behind Flame all bent and broken. The tomatoes were trampled and squashed. The bean trellis lay in a large heap.

"It's ruined!" said Sara. "My beautiful garden is ruined!"

Holly walked toward Flame very slowly. She clucked to her and held out her hand. Flame looked at Holly. But she kept right on munching.

"Come here, Flame," Holly urged. Flame turned and walked away. She wrecked another stalk of corn. "Now stop that!" Holly said. "Come back to your corral like a good girl."

But Flame ignored her. Every time Holly got near her, Flame retreated. She wasn't about to go back to her corral.

Just then, Butch came riding up on Tonto. "Butch! Get back!" Holly yelled. It was too late.

44

Flame took off running in a gallop. "Now see what you've done!" Holly yelled at him.

"I was just trying to help," Butch said.

"I was doing fine without you!" Holly cried.

"Stop it, kids," Pastor Hunter said.

They all watched as Flame ran around to the back side of the yard. They could watch her. But they couldn't catch her.

Suddenly, Flame saw the clothesline full of clean, white, flapping sheets. "Oh, no!" Sara Hunter cried out. "My laundry!"

Flame ran headlong into the sheets. The line was ripped from the poles! A string of sheets settled onto the back of the running horse. They trailed behind her and dragged in the grass and dirt all the way across the empty field.

"Look at the filly go!" Mr. Moffat yelled.

"My sheets!" cried Mrs. Hunter.

"My horse!" cried Holly.

Pastor Hunter started laughing. And he laughed and laughed. Then Mr. Moffat laughed. And Butch laughed. Everyone laughed, except Holly. She didn't think it was one bit funny.

"I still don't have my horse back," Holly said.

"Oh, just leave the gate open for her. Fill up her

feed bucket and maybe she'll wander back this evening," Mr. Moffat said through his laughter. "You won't get next to that horse today. She's spooked, and it'll take hours before she calms down."

"Look at the mess she made," said Holly's mother. Dirty laundry lay on the ground. A once-beautiful vegetable garden lay in ruins. And a long string of sheets was strung along the ground all the way to the far side of the meadow.

"Come on, Butch," Mr. Moffat said with a smile. "I think we'd better go on home now. There's nothing else we can do here."

Butch rode off on Tonto. Holly heard him say to himself, "Dumb horse!"

After they left, Holly turned to her dad. "I'm sorry," she said in a small voice.

"I know," he said. He put his arm around her shoulders. "But at least we know she's all right. She took off toward the woods. It's all fenced in back there. So she can't get off our property. We'll keep an eye out for her if she comes up this way toward the road. She'll be OK. Now go fill up her feed bucket and leave the gate open. Maybe she'll be home for supper."

Eight

But Flame did not come back for supper. And she didn't come back during the night. When Holly woke up the next morning, she hurried down to the corral. But Flame was not back and the feed bucket was untouched.

"Don't worry," her mother said at breakfast.

It was Sunday morning. Holly had to start getting ready for Sunday School and church. Soon the congregation from all over the area would be arriving for Sunday services.

Holly fidgeted the entire time during Sunday School class. She couldn't concentrate on the lesson. All she could think about was Flame. When her teacher asked her who was swallowed by a great fish, Holly couldn't even think of the answer.

Butch and the other kids snickered at her. But she didn't care. She just wanted Flame to come home.

47

During church, Holly sat by a window. She could see the corral from it. If Flame wandered back, Holly told herself, she could run outside and shut the gate behind her. It seemed like a good plan.

She listened as her mother led the choir in a beautiful song. Holly also tried to sing the hymns along with the congregation. But she kept looking out the window and losing her place in the hymnal.

Mrs. Moffat played the organ and the people sang. Pastor Hunter sat in the pulpit. Fresh air came in through the open doors and windows. It was a perfect summer day—bright and sunny and warm.

Suddenly, a gasp went up from the back of the church. Next, the choir stopped singing and started pointing. Then Pastor Hunter stood up and stared at the door.

Holly turned in her pew. There stood Flame. She was halfway inside the church. Her ears were pricked forward. The organ music! Of course, Flame had heard the organ music and had come to listen.

"Keep playing, Mrs. Moffat!" Pastor Hunter said aloud. "Everybody, please sit still and don't make any sudden moves. Holly, get a belt or something

and see if you can hook it through her halter."

Holly borrowed a belt from Mr. Jackson. Slowly she walked to the back of the church. Flame stood quietly. She was still listening to the music. "Please, don't let her run away again," Holly said to herself as she approached Flame. But Flame looked pretty tired. Holly walked right up to her.

"Hi, Flame," Holly said soothingly. "How are you? You like that music?" Then Holly reached up and looped the belt through the bottom of the halter. She had her! At last, Flame was captured!

Holly led her back out of the church and over to the corral. She led Flame into the corral, unlooped the belt and closed the gate behind her. Flame walked over to the feed bucket and started eating.

"She's back," Holly said. "Safe and sound. Thanks, God . . . and thanks, Mrs. Moffat, for your wonderful music."

* * * * * *

Naturally, it was the talk of the area for days. Most people thought it was pretty funny. A local newspaper reporter even came out to the house. He took pictures of Flame and talked with Pastor

Hunter and Holly.

The next day, there was a story in the paper with Holly and Flame's picture. "Horse Attends Local Church Service" the headline read. It told the whole story about Flame, the wild mustang, and how she'd gotten away and run through the garden, wrecked the clothesline and then showed up the next day for church service. "No doubt to repent" the reporter wrote.

It took a couple of weeks, but finally life got back to normal again. The summer was flying by, and Holly still hadn't ridden Flame once. "She'll never be ready for the Spring Festival," Holly told herself. So, she went to her dad one morning.

"Daddy, I think it's about time I tried to ride Flame," Holly told him. "She's very tame now. And I want to ride her."

Pastor Hunter put down his book. "You know, Holly," he said, "I think you're right. It's a good day for a ride. So why don't we go see if Flame will cooperate?"

Holly had been working with Flame all along. She and Patsy had taught Flame how to follow behind them when led by a rope. They had taught Flame to stop and start with a tug of the rope. And they had even put a saddle blanket across her back and leaned over her back.

Now, it was time to sit on her back. Holly felt very excited. But she was nervous, too. What if Flame threw her?

Pastor Hunter clipped on two ropes to Flame's halter. He tied the ropes to the fence rail. Holly slid the saddle blanket onto Flame's back. "So far, so good," Holly said.

"Are you ready for a leg up?" her dad asked.

"Ready," said Holly.

Pastor Hunter boosted Holly high and she swung her leg over Flame's back. Flame was startled. She had never felt any weight on her back before. She reared up. Holly slipped off and hit the ground.

"Are you all right?" Pastor Hunter asked.

"Sure," Holly said. She jumped up and patted Flame to calm her down. Holly fumbled in her pocket and brought out a sugar cube. Flame ate it.

"Ready to try again?" her dad asked.

Holly nodded, and he gave her another leg up. This time, Flame just jumped from side to side. Holly wrapped her fingers around Flame's mane hairs and pressed her knees hard into Flame's sides. She slid around a lot. But she didn't fall off.

Her dad talked softly to Flame and slowly she began to calm down. Holly patted Flame from atop her perch. "I'm on!" she cried. "I'm on my own horse."

"Good job, honey!" her dad said. "You've done it. You're on board a formerly wild mustang."

Holly was thrilled. Everything looked so different from the back of her horse. She looked down on her father and over the corral fence. It was a wonderful feeling.

Now, with some hard work, she'd teach Flame to run a barrel course. Next stop—the Spring Festival—and a Blue Ribbon!

Nine

The training of Flame went very smoothly. In no time at all, Holly was riding her around the corral bareback. Her dad watched until he was sure Holly could manage Flame by herself. Then Holly rode Flame all alone.

Holly felt like an Indian from the Old West. She sat high atop Flame and made her walk, run or gallop with voice commands and a gentle pressure from the rope reins attached to Flame's halter.

"To make her really obey, you'll have to get her used to a bit," Mr. Moffat told Holly one afternoon. He was watching Holly ride around the corral. "Once she's used to a bridle, bit and saddle, then you can ride her all over your property."

So that was the very next thing Holly and her dad worked on with Flame. Of course, Flame didn't like the bit in her mouth at all. But she did get used to it.

Mr. Moffat loaned Holly an old saddle of Tonto's

and Holly practiced saddling Flame. She had to put the saddle on Flame's back. Then she had to tighten the girth and make sure it was secure before she could ride. Yet Holly's favorite way to ride Flame was bareback.

"Are you ever going to get a new saddle?" Patsy asked as she watched Holly saddle up one morning.

"I hope so," Holly said. "I'd love a brand new saddle. All shiny and new. Maybe one with a silver horn." Holly's eyes were shining with the thought.

"I'll bet that would cost a lot," said Patsy.

"Yeah," Holly agreed. "But it's fun to think about. I'll bet we'd knock out the judges' eyes with a saddle like that!"

"And you could get a purple cowgirl shirt with pearl buttons," Patsy said excitedly.

"And a yellow bandanna to wear around my neck, said Holly.

"How about a white cowboy hat?"

"Sure. One with a real leather band. And new boots, too," Holly added. "Real black leather boots to match the new saddle with the silver horn."

Both girls started giggling. Holly knew she would never own such a saddle and clothes, but it was fun to pretend.

"What's so funny?" The question came from Butch Moffat. He had ridden up behind them on Tonto.

They looked up at him. "None of your business," Holly told him.

"Probably laughing about your horse," Butch said meanly. "She's such a runt and all."

"She is NOT!" said Holly. She swung up into the saddle.

"What ya gonna do?" he asked. "Ride your pony around her pony ring?" Then he laughed.

"We could outrun you anytime!" Holly said hotly.

"Fat chance!" said Butch. "Come out of your little ring and we'll have a race."

Boy, Holly thought, would I like to show him a thing or two! Instead she said, "I wouldn't want to embarrass you by winning."

It was the wrong thing to say. "Winning!" Butch said. "I could give you a head start and still beat you."

Holly tried to ignore him. But he made her angry. She was itching to race him. But she knew what her father would say. Flame had to be trained to obey her. Holly might not be able to control her if Flame got the bit in her teeth and kept on running.

Butch teased and taunted Holly more and more. She got madder and madder. "Just pay no attention to him," Patsy advised. Holly couldn't.

Finally she said, "All right, Butch. I'll race you. Patsy, open the gate."

"Do you think you should?" Patsy asked.

"I'll race him across the pasture and back. That should be fair enough. And after I beat him, he'll leave us in peace."

Patsy opened the gate. Holly's heart was pounding. She knew she shouldn't be doing this. "OK," Butch said. "We'll start from here. Patsy can yell, 'Go.'"

The two horses stood next to each other. Flame was nervous. She was dancing around. Holly was scared. What if she couldn't control Flame?

Suddenly, Patsy yelled "Go!" Butch was prepared and took off. Holly dug her heels into Flame's sides and yelled "Ya!" But Tonto already had a good head start.

Holly felt like she was flying! The grass was a green blur. She could see Tonto ahead and she urged Flame to run faster. The wind whipped her braids back and almost took her breath away. She could hear the sounds of Flame's hooves pounding

on the grassy ground.

She was gaining on Tonto. "Ya, Flame!" Holly yelled again. The wind carried her voice away. All at once, the pasture fence loomed ahead of them. Tonto turned effortlessly and started back.

Holly realized that Flame couldn't turn as quickly. Tonto was used to doing the barrel run. Flame wasn't. She wasn't trained to turn instantly like Tonto.

"Whoa!" Holly yelled. She pulled hard backwards

on the reins. Flame pulled herself up. Just in the instant before she would have collided with the fence, Flame came to a halt. Holly almost flipped over Flame's head. But she hung on.

Holly was shaking. She'd almost been thrown. And Flame had almost crashed into the fence! They both could have been seriously injured. All because Holly had let Butch make her angry. She felt very ashamed of herself. What if Flame had broken a leg? Or worse?

Slowly, Holly talked to Flame to calm her down. Then she turned Flame around and started back across the pasture toward the corral. Holly gritted her teeth. She'd just have to suffer through Butch's taunts.

She didn't have to worry about Butch, though. Standing next to the gate was her father. And he looked very angry.

* * * * * *

"Just what do you think you were doing, young lady?" Pastor Hunter sat in the big chair in his study. He asked the question again.

Holly hung her head and stared at her feet. "I

don't know," she said quietly.

"Don't you know that you could have hurt yourself or Flame? That you took an awful chance?"

"Yes," Holly said. "I'm very sorry, Daddy. I-I just let Butch get me angry. When he said Flame was a runt and he could beat her in a race . . ."

"So you thought you'd prove him wrong. Is that it?"

Holly nodded. Her dad said, "I should forbid you to ride her at all. I should turn her back to the government."

"Oh, please don't, Dad!" Holly cried. "I really am sorry! I'll never do anything like that again!"

"You bet you won't!" Pastor Hunter said firmly. "Do you still want to train her to run barrel races?" he asked.

"Yes. I sure do. Then I can beat Butch and not get me or Flame hurt," Holly said.

"Then I suggest you concentrate on doing that— instead of trying to run her legs off."

"Yes, sir," Holly said. "I promise. No more races. Just hard work on learning to run the barrel course."

Ten

It was Labor Day. Holly hopped out of bed early. And even though she knew that school was starting back the next day, nothing could dampen her excitement.

Today was the church's wonderful Labor Day Picnic. Everyone in the congregation came from miles around for this event. Everyone! It was the biggest, most fun day of the year—next to Christmas. Holly could hardly wait for the day to get started.

Her mother had been cooking for days. She'd fixed fried chicken, potato salad, lemonade, biscuits, two pies and a cake. Yum! Holly was ready to start eating.

And best of all, Holly was going to ride Flame to the picnic. All of the food tables were set up on the far side of the church building. There were trees and large grassy areas where people could spread their blankets and eat.

Foot races, sack races, and three-legged races were all planned for the day. And Pastor Hunter had said that Holly could take some of the younger kids for a ride on Flame. "Oh, boy! Oh, boy!" Holly said out loud. Then she hurried and got dressed.

Later that day, Holly sat next to Patsy under a tree in the shade. Flame grazed nearby. Becky Collins played her guitar and sang songs for the younger kids.

"I think I ate too much," Patsy groaned.

"I know I did," Holly said and spread out on her back. "But isn't it a wonderful picnic?"

Patsy burped. They both laughed. "Think you'll be ready for the sack race in an hour?" Holly asked her.

"Sure," Patsy nodded. "Maybe I need another piece of Mrs. Elam's cake for extra energy," she suggested.

"Patsy, you'll bust!" Holly laughed.

"Probably."

Just then the air was filled by the voice of Butch Moffat. "Hi ya, freckles!"

Holly turned in time to see him dismount from Tonto and plop down on the grass beside her. "This is a private party," Holly told him.

"Private, *smi*-vate," he said. "School starts tomorrow. Did you pass to the fifth grade?"

"Of course, dummy," Holly said. "Did you?"

"Sure. So you know what that means?"

Holly waited for him to say something. "It means," he went on, "that we'll be in the same class again since there's only one fifth-grade class."

Holly made a face at him. "I know. Maybe I'll wear black tomorrow."

Butch poked her with his elbow. "I won another trophy last week at the Jaycee's Rodeo. Tonto did their barrel run in just nineteen seconds."

"Terrific," Holly said flatly.

"Think you and Flame will ever get good enough to compete against me?"

Holly felt her temper rising again. "Someday we'll beat you," she said.

"Who you gonna ride—Patsy?" Butch teased.

"Get lost!" Patsy said and shoved him. Butch dropped over, laughing hysterically.

"Flame and I will beat you," Holly continued. "In fact, next spring, at the Spring Festival, Flame and I will beat you in any barrel race event you want to enter."

Butch stopped laughing. "Hey! You're serious,

aren't you?"

"You bet!" Holly said.

"Good!" Butch said, jumping to his feet and climbing up on Tonto. "Then it's a bet. Because you have no chance against me and Tonto. No chance at all."

After he'd ridden away, Patsy turned to Holly. "Do you think you should have said anything to him so soon? I mean, the Spring Festival is months away, and you haven't really started training yet."

"Yes, I have," Holly said. "But now I need you to help me. Every day after school and on Saturdays, we need to work with Flame . . ."

"Hey!" Patsy said with a start. "Speaking of Flame—where'd she go?"

Holly bounded up and looked around. Sure enough, Flame was nowhere in sight. While she'd been busy talking to Butch, Flame had wandered away. "Oh, no," Holly said. "Quick, Patsy, we've got to find her right now."

Both girls took off running. Holly passed by blankets full of picnicing families. Babies were asleep in play pens, grown-ups were stretched out on blankets, small groups of women were sitting and talking. From far away, Holly could hear the sounds of the father-son softball game.

Lazy butterflies fluttered in the hot summer air and one lone squirrel scurried up an oak tree. Holly looked left and right. But she couldn't see Flame anywhere. Dad will kill me! she thought. "You lost a horse!" she imagined hearing him say.

Suddenly Holly heard a shriek. It came from the direction of the food tables. Holly hurried faster. Just then she saw Flame.

The red pony had discovered the dessert table. Mrs. Elam was screeching, "Shoo! Go away! Shoo, shoo!" She was waving a tiny white handkerchief at Flame. But Flame ignored her.

Instead, Flame helped herself to Mrs. Moffat's luscious strawberry cake. It was heaped with red berries and cream. Flame had eaten a huge chunk right smack out of the top of the cake and was licking the mounds of whipped cream from off her nose.

"Oh, my goodness!" Holly cried and ran over to the table. She snatched Flame by the reins and tried to pull her back. "Bad horse!" Holly scolded.

"Get that creature out of here!" Mrs. Elam demanded.

"Oh, yes! Yes!" Holly said. "I'm so sorry. She just

loves sweets. It's all my fault! I'm sorry!"

People seemed to appear from everywhere. Everyone stood there pointing and talking at once. Someone started laughing. Someone else called out, "At least Flame has good taste."

Holly wished she could fall into a hole in the ground. She'd never been so embarrassed. Flame kept licking the cream off her nose with her long pick tongue.

Holly heard her father's deep voice. "I might have known," he said with a sigh.

Holly smiled up at him weakly. "She likes cake, too," she said. By now, almost the entire congregation was standing around staring at them. Most people were laughing. Holly smiled a little. It *was* funny. But she was almost glad school was starting tomorrow. She needed a "vacation" away from Flame.

Eleven

Once school started, Holly found herself very busy. She had a lot of school work to do every day. She still had to do her daily chores. And she had to take care of Flame. It was hard to find extra time to train Flame to run a barrel course.

But she and Patsy got some old, worn out traffic cones from the Highway Department. Holly had written the Mayor and asked for them. Then she and Patsy set up the traffic cones in Flame's corral and began walking Flame around them.

First, Holly and Flame would walk through the course. Next, they would trot through the course. Finally, they tried running through the course. The trick was not to knock over any of the cones. It was hard to do! But slowly, Holly and Flame improved their efforts until they worked good together as a team. Patsy timed Flame's runs with a stopwatch because Flame had to run fast and accurately.

Every time Flame did a very good job, Holly rewarded her with apples and sugar cubes.

Autumn turned into winter and the snows came. The girls could no longer practice very much. So they decided to wait until spring before training again. Since the Spring Festival was always the first of May, Holly felt she had plenty of time.

* * * * * *

Flame seemed very happy in her farm home. She grew fat during the long winter months. Her coat also grew long and shaggy. It protected her from the harsh winds of winter. And when it got too cold, Flame always went inside her little stall for extra protection.

As the winter wore on, Holly grew, too. One cold morning she looked at her calendar. It was already March. Holly realized with surprise that it was almost time for her birthday. She was almost eleven years old.

The fifth of March dawned sunny and cold. Holly hurried down the stairs. "Hi!" her mother said. She gave Holly a big hug and said, "Happy Birthday!" Holly beamed. In the evening there would be cake and ice cream and lots of presents. She could hardly wait!

At school Patsy gave her a box wrapped with pink flowered paper.

"For me?" Holly asked.

"Open it," Patsy said. "I bought it with my own money."

Holly was excited as she tore off the paper. She opened the box. Inside was the most beautiful cowgirl shirt Holly had ever seen. "It's BEAUTI-FUL!" Holly cried.

"Thanks," Patsy said. "I picked it out just for you."

The shirt was bright red. "It's got real imitation pearl buttons!" Patsy smiled.

"Oh, thank you! Thank you!" Holly cried. All the other girls gathered around Holly's desk and admired the shirt. Even some of the boys looked it over. Butch Moffat was out sick with the flu. So Holly counted that as his birthday present to her.

That night, at home, Holly wore the shirt to her family birthday party. Her mom and dad thought it was very nice, too. After her mother had cleared the table, she brought in Holly's special cake. Her mom had decorated it like a corral. A plastic horse was perched on top of the cake. "That's Flame," her mom told Holly.

Holly listened while they sang to her. Then she closed her eyes and made a wish. And finally she blew out every one of the eleven candles with just one breath.

"I think there just might be a present around here someplace for you," her dad said, looking under the table. "No, it's not there. Hm-m . . . Where did I put that box?"

"You're teasing me!" Holly said. "Where did you hide my present?"

"I know!" he said, snapping his fingers. "It's in my study." Holly jumped up from the table and ran to his study. Sure enough, there in the middle of his desk was a huge box. Holly couldn't even lift it. It was too heavy.

"Think you can get it open?" her mother asked.

Holly stared wide-eyed at it. What could it be? It was so large. She tore off the wrappings and lifted the lid. Inside was a saddle.

"Oh, my!" Holly gasped. "A brand new saddle!"

Her dad lifted it out of the box. He laid it on the floor. The saddle was light brown and had all kinds of western carvings on it. It had new wooden stirrups, too. There was also a matching bridle and a beautiful new saddle blanket. Her new saddle didn't have a silver horn, but Holly thought it was the most beautiful saddle in the world.

Holly was so happy that she felt like crying. She couldn't say "Thank you" enough. "It's the most wonderful birthday I ever had!" Holly said. And she hugged her mom and dad. "Now I can ride in the Spring Festival in real style," Holly told them.

"The Spring Festival?" Pastor Hunter asked.

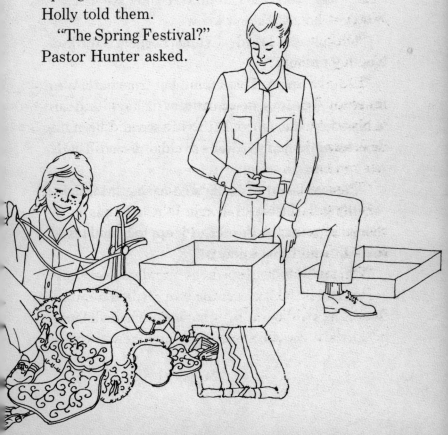

"Don't tell me you still want to ride in the barrel run?"

"Oh, yes!" Holly nodded. "More than ever."

"But, Holly, Flame's not ready for that. Why, most of the horses in that event have been doing it for years. You've hardly practiced."

"But, Dad, I'll practice harder than ever once it's a little warmer. And Flame is very fast. And she learns fast, too. We can do it. I know we can."

"Gee, honey, I don't know . . ."

"Oh, please, Daddy," Holly begged. "We'll do good. I promise."

"But the Spring Festival is miles from here. We'd have to stay in a hotel. And we'd have to board Flame in a special stall at the Festival. The riding competitions happen over a five-day period. There's so much to do to enter the events."

"Please, Daddy," Holly said again. "More than anything in the world, I want to ride Flame in the barrel races at the Festival. Please help me. I know we can win. I just know it!"

Twelve

Holly had never seen so much activity and excitement. This was the Spring Festival. There were people, animals, cars, vans and trailers everywhere she looked. She heard noises from goats, pigs, cows and horses. Every breed of farm animal had its own special tent or area. Owners and Festival officials ran around making sure that pens and stalls were locked. They made sure the animals had enough food and water.

In the stable area where Flame was safely kept, Holly sat down on a bale of hay and tried to catch her breath. What a frantic couple of days! But at last they were here. Holly, Flame, Pastor and Mrs. Hunter—all of them ready and waiting for the great Spring Festival to begin.

Holly was a little nervous. She and Flame had practiced and practiced. In the corral back home, Flame could run any course Holly and Patsy could make up. But what about here? With all the people? And the lights and noise from the Festival? Could Flame concentrate and run the race for all the judges?

"Penny for your thoughts?" Pastor Hunter asked as he walked over to where Holly was sitting.

She smiled at him. "Oh, I was just wondering if Flame will be too excited to run in the barrel race event," she said.

"Well, that event isn't for another two days. She'll have time to adjust to her new surroundings," her dad said.

Holly looked over at Flame. She was munching on some hay. She didn't look very interested in anything except her supper.

"I guess you're right," Holly sighed. "Where's Mom?"

"She went over to the homemaking exhibits," Pastor Hunter told Holly. "There are some interesting quilts on display and she wanted to see them. If you're sure Flame is all settled in, we'll go on over and join Mom. Maybe we can get some dinner and then play some of the games."

"Great!" Holly said, hopping down from the bale of hay. Holly loved all the excitement at the

Festival. There were lots of games and prizes to win. There were all kinds of interesting foods and even more interesting people. "We'll be back later, Flame," Holly told her horse. Flame only scooped another large mouthful of hay and chewed it.

* * * * * *

It was a beautiful spring day. Holly led Flame out of her stall and walked her around the stable area and paddock. Many other owners were also walking their horses for exercise.

There were so many horses! Palaminos, quarter horses, appaloosas, pintos—every breed of horse Holly had ever read about. Some were there for riding events. Others were there for the special saddle events. Still others, like Holly, were there for the rodeo events. Holly tried to pick out who might be riding in the children's division of the barrel races.

"So you really did come and bring that pony of yours."

Holly stopped dead in her tracks. The voice was Butch Moffat's. Holly turned and saw Butch sitting on top of Tonto. "I said I would," Holly said.

"Didn't you believe me?"

"I didn't think you'd have the guts," Butch teased.

Holly ignored him and marched off with Flame. "We got in late last night," Butch explained as he rode along beside her. "And guess what? We're in the stall right next to yours!"

Holly stared up at him. Oh, no! It couldn't be true. Wasn't she ever going to get rid of Butch?

"What're you gonna do now?" Butch asked.

Holly tied the rope on Flame's halter to a post next to the watering trough and reached in her back jeans pocket for the curry brush. "Groom my horse," Holly said. Then she added, "And I don't need an audience."

Flame began to drink and Holly began to brush her soft red coat. Butch slid down off Tonto's back and stood next to Holly.

"So, you think you can beat me?" he asked with smirk.

Holly said nothing. Butch went on. "Don't you know that Tonto has run this event four times and took first place twice, second place once and third once?"

"Ancient history," Holly said while she brushed.

She was determined that she wasn't going to let Butch make her angry.

He laughed aloud. "History repeats itself," he said.

"Well, maybe not this time!" Holly said, ducking under Flame's neck and going to the other side.

Butch walked around and stood in front of Flame's head. She'd finished drinking and had backed up from the water trough. "Is she your horse yet?" he asked.

Holly kept brushing Flame's coat until it gleamed. "No, not yet," she said. "But she will be in just a couple more weeks. I know the vet will certify that I've taken good care of her," Holly added.

"Maybe if you're lucky, he won't," Butch laughed. "Then you can ship her back to Wyoming and get yourself a real horse." Butch threw back his head and laughed hard.

"You stop that!" Holly demanded. She was getting angrier. Why did Butch always make her so mad?

Just then Flame started sniffing at Butch's front shirt pocket. "Hey!" he yelled. "Cut that out!" But Flame kept right on sniffing.

"She smells something," Holly explained and

tried to pull Flame's head away from Butch's chest. But Flame only pulled back. Her pink tongue reached out and licked Butch's pocket.

"Stop that!" he yelled again.

"What's in your pocket?" Holly asked, tugging on Flame's rope.

"Sugar for Tonto," he said. "Don't, horse!" Butch shouted. He put his hand over his pocket. Then he made the big mistake of stepping backwards. Butch forgot that he was standing right in front of the water trough. The backs of his legs hit the rim of the trough. "Oh-oh-oh!" he cried as he lost his balance.

Splash! Butch hit the water and went completely under the surface. He came up sputtering. Holly started laughing. She couldn't help herself.

"Y-Y-You . . .!" Butch sputtered. "You'll be sorry! You did that on purpose!"

"Did not!" Holly said between her laughs. "Flame thought of it all by herself. Maybe you'll be nicer to her now." Then Holly untied Flame and led her back to her stall. She left Butch sputtering and soaking wet in the middle of the water trough.

Thirteen

"Ladies and gentlemen! The Spring Festival Rodeo proudly announces the Barrel Obstacle Course Racing Event! Will the contestants and their horses please prepare to compete?" The announcer's voice boomed over the loudspeaker through the hot afternoon air.

Holly smiled nervously up at her father and clutched Flame's reins tightly. This was it. The event Holly had been waiting for for almost one year—the Barrel Race of the Spring Festival.

"You ready?" Pastor Hunter asked.

"Sure," Holly said. "Is my number straight?" She turned to show him the bold black cardboard sign pinned to her back. Her sign said Twelve. Holly was one of twenty-two kids riding in this event. She would be the twelfth one to run the course.

She looked around the crowd of people and saw Butch already mounted on Tonto's back. He was wearing number nine. He also was ignoring her.

The stands were filled with people who had come to watch an entire afternoon of rodeo events. Holly searched for her mom in the crowds, but there were just too many people. Holly couldn't find her. One by one, the riders began to file into the rodeo arena for the Parade of Contestants. Holly hoisted herself up on Flame and prepared to ride through the open gate and into the dusty arena.

"Good luck," her dad called. "I'll be praying for you!"

She smiled back at him and took a deep breath. Then she took her place in line behind the contestant who wore number eleven. Music played over the loudspeakers. One by one the announcer called out their names and the names of their horses. Holly was wide-eyed. There were so many people watching them! And it was so exciting to be there, riding slowly around the arena, waving to everybody.

"... Butch Moffat up on Tonto ..." she heard the announcer say. The crowd let up a big cheer. It was clear that Butch was going to be a favorite with the audience. "... And number twelve is Holly Hunter on board Flame ..." Holly had never heard her name announced before. It was very thrilling.

Finally, everyone had been introduced. They filed back out of the arena and waited while cowboys set up the course with big heavy barrels. It was going to be a difficult course. Holly prayed that she and Flame could run it in the best time and without knocking over any of the barrels.

Then the loudspeaker announced rider number one. A small dark-haired boy on a chestnut-colored horse rode up to the start line. Holly swallowed hard. The flagman suddenly dropped his flag, and the boy and horse took off in a gallop. He raced around barrel after barrel. The crowd cheered. But at the top of the course his horse suddenly leaned too far into one of the barrels and knocked it over. That meant that even if he made good time, points would be deducted by the judges for a fault.

"Ten more to go," Holly said to herself. She rubbed Flame's neck. Holly squirmed in her new saddle and adjusted her bandanna for the fiftieth time. "Nine more to go," she said as the second contestant finished.

As Holly watched, she began to see where some of the riders were making mistakes. If they ran too fast, they knocked over some barrels. If they didn't knock over any barrels, then they ran too slowly. The trick was to keep an even pace and not to cut too sharply at the top of the course. Holly planned her strategy in her mind.

"Butch Moffat and Tonto!" the announcer called. Holly looked over at Butch. The crowd cheered. He had a look of total concentration on his face. Suddenly the flagman dropped the flag.

"Yah!" Butch shouted and dug his heels into Tonto's sides. Tonto took off like a shot. The audience clapped as Tonto galloped smoothly around each barrel. At the top of the course, Butch turned Tonto sharply to the left. Tonto managed the turn and brushed up against the barrel. It rocked, but it didn't fall. Everyone clapped as Tonto thundered down the stretch.

"Seventeen seconds flat!" the voice on the loudspeaker said. Holly's heart lurched. Butch's time was three-and-a-half seconds faster than any other rider who'd run the course. A cheer went up from the crowd. Seventeen seconds! Could she and Flame beat it? Holly honestly didn't know.

Holly watched the next two riders run the course. Neither came close to Butch's time. Then suddenly the announcer called out her name. It was her turn.

Holly went over her strategy in her mind one more time and then rode out into the rodeo arena.

Flame snorted and pawed the ground. "Easy!" Holly said. She pulled back firmly on the reins. It would be important to get off to a fast start. Holly watched the flagman from the corner of her eye.

"Ready?" he asked.

Holly nodded and leaned forward in her saddle. The flag dropped. "Yah!" Holly yelled. Flame leaped forward like a shot.

She took the first barrel easily. Then she galloped toward the second barrel. The pace was good. Flame cut in and out between every barrel perfectly. The top of the course loomed ahead. Holly knew she'd have to make this part perfect . . . *and* fast.

Holly pulled Flame abruptly left. Flame responded beautifully. Then she turned her sharply to the right. Holly felt the edge of the barrel brush her foot. It teetered, but it didn't fall. Flame rounded the last barrel and raced for home. The wind whipped back Holly's braids as she galloped for the finish line. Holly pulled Flame's reins back to stop her as Flame crossed the line.

Holly tried to catch her breath and listen for her official time. There was a long pause. "Holly

Hunter," the voice began, "and Flame. A new record! Fifteen and four-tenths of a second! Congratulations!"

"Yahoo!" Holly yelled. She leaned over and threw her arms around Flame's neck. "We did it!" she shouted.

People came over and patted her on the back. "Good job!" they said. "Well done."

Holly knew she hadn't won yet. There were still eleven more riders to go. But it seemed unlikely that anyone could beat her time. She watched and waited as the other contestants ran the course. None did as well as Holly.

Finally it was over. Holly and Flame were the official winners! Butch and Tonto were second. She was so excited! "We won!" Holly told Flame over and over.

It was time for the Parade of Champions. One by one the winners of all the kid's rodeo events rode out into the big rodeo arena to receive their trophies and ribbons.

Holly sat tall and proud on Flame's back waiting for her name to be called. When it was called, she rode forward and took the silver trophy the judge handed up to her. "Thanks!" Holly said. Then the

judge pinned a big
blue ribbon on to Flame's bridle.
It was the happiest moment of Holly's life.

She rode Flame back into the Champion lineup
and looked over at Butch. Tonto had a large red
ribbon pinned to his bridle. Holly felt very proud of
Flame and not one bit mean toward Butch.

Funny, she thought. I don't even feel like rubbing
it in. She was just happy she'd won. It was a dream
come true. And right then Holly loved the whole
world—even Butch Moffat.

Fourteen

"It's beautiful!" Patsy said, staring at the trophy. "I sure wish I could have seen you win it."

Holly and Patsy stood in Holly's kitchen and looked over all the stuff Holly had brought back with her from the Festival. Holly showed Patsy the rodeo program with her name printed in it. She showed her the First Place ribbon of Flame's. She showed her the trophy, the number Holly had worn on her back, and even the stuffed dog Pastor Hunter had won for her at the Festival.

"It was terrific!" Holly said.

"Are you going to go again next year?" Patsy asked.

"You bet," Holly nodded.

Just then, they heard a car horn honk from outside.

The girls looked at each other. "Mrs. Moffat," they said in unison. Holly went over to the door and looked out. Sure enough, Mrs. Moffat and Butch had pulled up. They got out of the car and walked up to the porch.

"Hello!" Mrs. Moffat called. "Anybody home?"

"Come in," Holly smiled. "Mom's over at the church going through old music books," Holly explained.

"Then I'll just head on over there," said Mrs. Moffat. "Butch, why don't you stay here with the girls and swap horse stories?" She patted Butch on his blond head. He rolled his eyes and shuffled from foot to foot.

After she left, the three kids just stood around staring at the floor and walls. Holly couldn't think of a thing to say to Butch.

"So, what do you think of Holly's 'little pony' now?" Patsy asked.

"Aw . . . she's OK," Butch said.

"OK!" Holly snapped. "She's more than OK. She's super. And you know it."

Butch looked down his nose at Holly. "She won one race. Big deal. The trick is to keep winning," he said.

Holly felt her blood boil. "We'll beat you anytime you want!" she shouted. She stamped her foot.

"Honestly, Butch Moffat! Sometimes you make me
so MAD!"

Butch grinned at her. Then he reached over and
tugged on one of her long braids. "I know!" he
smiled and then ran out the kitchen door.

* * * * * *

"Holly, would you please stop fidgeting?" Sara
Hunter said.

Holly tried to sit still in the living room chair, but

91

she couldn't—not when her dad and the veterinarian were out in the corral with Flame.

This was the day Holly had waited for with both dread and excitement. This was the day that an official doctor looked at Flame and certified her good health. Once and for all, Flame would become her horse—IF the vet agreed that the Hunters had taken good care of her.

"I don't know why you're worried," her mom said. "You've done a wonderful job with Flame. It's just a formality. He'll sign that form for the government, and Flame will be yours forever."

Holly smiled at her mother. She knew her mom was trying to make her feel better. And deep in her heart, Holly knew that no one could have loved Flame more or treated her better than she had. But, it still wasn't official yet. And until the vet signed the form, it wouldn't be official.

Finally, her dad came into the room. He waved a piece of paper in the air. "We got it!" he beamed.

"Yea!" Holly shouted. She threw her arms around him. "I knew we would! Flame's mine! All mine!"

"You knew it all along?" Sara Hunter teased.

"Well . . . almost all along," Holly said. "I know!" Holly shouted. "Let's go down to the corral and tell

Flame together."

"Why not?" Pastor Hunter said. And taking them both by the hands, he led Holly and her mom outside.

They reached the corral. Holly whistled for Flame. The small red mustang came trotting over to the fence. She sniffed at Holly's pocket.

"You sugar thief," Holly laughed. She reached into her pocket and held out a lump of sugar. Flame took it.

"You know," Pastor began. "Mr. Moffat came to me yesterday with an interesting idea."

"What's that?" Holly asked.

"He said he was very impressed with Flame's performance in the rodeo. He said she was very fast and thought that her mustang bloodlines would be a real asset when she foals."

"You mean has a baby?" Mrs. Hunter asked.

"Yes. Anyway, he suggested that we consider letting her have a foal in about three years. I talked to the vet about it, and he thought it was a good idea. By then she'll be seven and ready to retire from barrel racing."

"Really!" Holly cried. "Oh, I can't wait."

"Mr. Moffat also suggested that we consider

93

Tonto as a sire for Flame's foal."

"What?" Holly shouted.

"What's wrong with that?" Pastor Hunter asked. "Tonto is a proven champion. I think he and Flame would have a fine foal."

"B-B-But . . ." Holly sputtered. "If that happens, Butch will be around here more than ever!"

"How about that?" her dad said. "You two might have to try and get along."

"That means we'll be . . . related!" Holly wailed.

Her parents laughed. "Holly," Mrs. Hunter said, putting her arm around Holly's shoulders. "In three more years you and Butch will both be fourteen years old."

"So?" Holly said.

"So, believe it or not, when you're fourteen, being around Butch will not be so unpleasant for you."

"Never!" Holly said. She turned and reached over the fence and hugged Flame. "If Flame has a foal, I know I'll love it. Even if I have to put up with Butch," she added.

Her mom just smiled. Holly blushed. And Flame nuzzled Holly's pocket, looking for one more lump of sugar.

94